WOODY AND JUNE VERSUS THE DARING RESCUE

WOODY AND JUNE VERSUS THE DARING RESCUE

WOODY AND JUNE VERSUS THE APOCALYPSE, EPISODE 7

ROBERT J. MCCARTER

LITTLE HUMMINGBIRD PUBLISHING

WOODY AND JUNE

VERSUS

THE APOCALYPSE

Woody and June versus the Daring Rescue

Woody and June versus the Apocalypse, Episode 7

Cover photography © Pancaketom | Dreamstime.com

"Zombies Ahead" image by ducu59us

Version 1.0, September 2019

ISBN: 978-1-941153-21-5

Find out more about this book at: WoodyAndJune.com

Visit Robert's website at: www.RobertJMcCarter.com

Published by:

Little Hummingbird Publishing

P.O. Box 23518

Flagstaff, AZ 86002

www.LittleHummingbird.com

Little Hummingbird Publishing is a division of Arapas, Inc. Find more about Arapas at: www.Arapas.com.

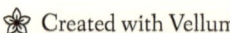 Created with Vellum

CHAPTER ONE

I WANT to confess to Dallas… all of my sins, even things that June doesn't know about, and there's a lot June doesn't know about. We've avoided talking much about our pre-apocalypse lives.

Dallas and I are walking at a good clip down Route 64 along the edge of the Grand Canyon, heading east from Lipan Point over to Desert View Overlook where the truck is parked (at least I hope it's still there). Dallas and I are friends. I trust her now, despite our rocky start, but our silent march under the starry glow of the Milky Way has given me too much time to think.

June taken by the psychotic, petty, wannabe warlord Talia, who just happens to be her ex. The challenges Dallas and I have to overcome before even getting our shot at getting her back, and the poor odds of it working out. Even if we do succeed, then what? The three of us trying to find a place far away from the zombies to live in peace, grow some food… That's not going to be easy.

I pat the pocket of my faded army surplus jacket. It's tied to my pack, so I have to twist my arm around. The seed packets are still there, the future is being able to grow food far away from the living and the undead. I adjust my Diamondbacks baseball cap and trot for a few steps, the backpack rattling on my back. Dallas has gotten ahead of me a bit.

It's a cool spring night at seven thousand feet, but cool feels good. There's a slight breeze, the air faintly scented by the juniper trees along the road. Our steps on the blacktop seem loud, ominous.

Dallas has a flashlight out and she's straight backed, a determined silhouette, her footfalls metronomic in their regularity.

I clear my throat, my mouth dry, but I can't get any words out. I want to tell her, like I told June, about when I was six and I accidentally shot my four-year-old brother Joshua in the arm. I want to tell her about the mess in Phoenix and what I did—or rather didn't do—and what it caused... well, what it cost, which is some good people their lives. It's the event that caused me to leave Phoenix and the psychotic, petty, wannabe warlord I had been following there.

And yes, I left because he was petty and psychotic, but more because every time I saw his lean face and grey eyes, I remembered what I didn't do.

I want to confess.

I clear my throat again, trying to find the words to even start the conversation.

"Somethin' on your mind, Beckman?" Dallas asks, her pace not varying, her head pointed forward.

I nod, although she can't see it. I'm not a religious guy, and if I had been, I don't think my faith would have survived the zombie apocalypse. But some of these things feel like sins, like blots on my soul. Infected wounds that need to be cleaned out.

"The past..." I mumble. "Just thinking about the past."

"The past is shit," she says.

Our hustle has erased the elation we felt and the camaraderie of escaping the Grand Canyon and Phantom Company alive.

And the past *is* shit, full of Zs, psychotic, petty, wannabe warlords, and cowards. The latter being my category.

And if you're reading this—if anyone gets to read this—you might think that insane considering what I've done since meeting June. And

I get that, but I don't feel it. What I do now doesn't erase what I didn't do in Phoenix.

"You know..." Dallas says a few minutes later, "that angsty funk pouring out of you right now is not going to help us get June back. Quite the opposite, you know."

She stops and faces me, the flashlight on the dirty pavement, but there's enough light for me to see her face. It's intense, but there is a whisper of compassion there.

"I've... I..." I shake my head and take a deep breath. "Some bad shit went down in Phoenix and my inaction cost some good people their lives."

The words come out in a rush, but I don't feel any better, that wasn't a confession, not really.

Dallas bites her thumbnail and slowly nods. She doesn't tell me the bad things she's done. She doesn't tell me that because of the Zs all sins are forgiven. She's got a few years on me, but given how wild she can be, I didn't really expect such a measured response from her.

She rubs her face, the fatigue suddenly showing. She slowly turns in a circle shining the flashlight around the perimeter. At first, I think she's looking for Zs, but she's not. "You and me," she says when she's facing me again. "It's just us out here. No Zs. None of our petty, peculiar warlords. Right?"

I nod, not sure where she's going and crack the smallest of smiles. I've said "psychotic, petty, wannabe warlord" over and over but she never seems to remember it.

"We're humans. We're alive. Right?" she continues.

I nod again.

"I've seen that look on your face before, Beckman. Talia, when she was trying to woo me, seemed to think that opening up to me would create some kind of a bond. She told me all about Albuquerque."

Her face darkens and she looks down. "She's got Albuquerque. You've got Phoenix. I've got that shit I pulled on you and June and much worse. We all have to find a way to live in the present and *live* with our past. No damn magic formula there."

She sighs, turns, and starts walking down the road.

"But..." I say as I catch up to her and fall in line beside her. "But, what does that mean?"

She snorts. "It means you're human, Beckman. And it also means I don't want to hear all your shit. Save that for your girlfriend once we rescue her, because I'm not your priest and I'm not your girlfriend, and we haven't been friends long enough for that."

I'm silent, chewing it over.

"Got it?" she asks, her voice just a bit too high.

"Yes. Got it." And I do get it. Hearing it would be a burden and we have enough burdens right now. It might be the proverbial straw for Dallas. If I told her, it would be all about me, not about her.

But I want to confess, because I'm afraid that if I don't do it now I won't have another chance.

I take a deep breath and shake it off.

First we get June back.

Then we find a place to survive.

And then we can try to heal.

CHAPTER TWO

THE TRUCK IS in the Desert View parking lot. I am so happy to see it that I almost cry. A brand-new—at the time of the apocalypse—crew-cab, jet-black Toyota pickup truck. Just the kind of truck I always wanted, but could never afford.

The keys are under the floor mat. It starts right up. There's gas in the tank and extra in jerry cans in the bed. We shuck our packs, hop in, and get going.

I pull out of the lot and get us back on 64 heading east towards Cameron. The cab is a bit stuffy and we roll the windows down, letting the wind blow through.

Years from now, if humanity recovers from the zombie apocalypse and something comes of this scribbling I've been doing and the efforts of June, Dallas, and myself, I wonder how I'll be viewed.

I've got a big mouth, but not like Dallas. I'm not the best fighter, that would be June. I'm brash and daring, but decidedly mild compared to the mercurial Dallas. And I'm not the smartest. June, once you get to know her, has a very sharp mind.

Even in emotional intelligence, I'm a distant third. They both seem to be able to read me like an open book.

So what am I compared to these two strong women?

Lucky comes to mind. Never bored, that's certainly true. Driven to be worthy of their companionship, without a doubt. Not good enough... yeah, there it is. This is what I fear. I've got my baggage and flaws which seem so big next to theirs. But, then again, I'm the one stuck in my head, so I can hope they don't see my flaws as clearly as I do.

I do think, though, that the one thing I bring to the table is my strange way of thinking. Taking little pieces of things (either literally or figuratively) and pulling them into something useful.

And BS. I'm pretty good at the BS.

"Time to tell me the plan?" Dallas asks, her voice loud, rising above the wind whipping through the cab.

It's dark, the headlights only catching glimpses of the desert, rocks and scraggly bushes whipping by. I've been down this road, there were no wrecks before, so we're going fast. We need to get as far as we can before the sun comes up.

We've lost some elevation and eased into the desert. The night is nice, in the low fifties.

I clear my throat. "The plan requires electronics, at least one drone, explosives, and an epic amount of BS. And caffeine, lots of caffeine."

She nods. "So Best Buy is for the drone and electronics. What about the explosives?"

I shake my head. "No clue, really. I'm thinking after we have everything else, we'll head east on I-40. They always seemed to be working on bridges out that way. I quickly searched one site when June was captured before, but it could be worth a second look. I've got a few other ideas."

I've been thinking about explosives quite a bit since June and my encounter with the Mount Elden psychotic, petty, wannabe warlord. It's valuable stuff in this new world and I think there are probably quite a few places to find it if you know where to look. Besides road construction, mining is a major use of explosives.

Dallas and I have been lucky so far, and I'm afraid that luck is going to run out before we get to June.

"And your psycho warlord friend?" she asks.

I shrug. "Keep your fingers crossed."

"Always, Beckman. Always."

CHAPTER THREE

ELDEN LOOKOUT TOWER sits on the southeastern portion of Mount Elden, right above the east side of Flagstaff with a great view of the big box stores behind the mall, including Best Buy, Home Depot, as well as I-40 heading east.

The psychotic, petty, wannabe warlord—we didn't get his name, I thought of him as "Mr. Short and Stocky" and June thought of him as "Asshole"—has a camp up there and mans the tower. I am quite sure that I'm on the "shoot on sight" list, so Flagstaff is not a friendly place, but the only place in the area with the kinds of stores we need.

On the way into town, while it's still dark, I change my mind and route around side roads with headlights off and get onto I-40 east and drive out to the ancient, crumbling Twin Arrows Trading Post.

The beat-up Ford Focus June and I used in our escape from Mr. Short and Stocky is still there, including my faux suicide vest. We get out, approach slowly, and circle the building before I go to the car.

We are hidden from Elden, so I turn on a flashlight, pull out the vest, and watch Dallas's eyes widen. The vest has what looks like thirty sticks of dynamite strapped to it with nails and screws glued to the sticks. There's wires and a dangling dead man's switch.

"What the..." she gasps.

I smile and yell, "Catch!" and toss her the vest.

She curses and dances out of the way, thinking I just threw a bunch of dynamite at her.

"It's fake," I say, laughing.

"Shit, Beckman! Shit!" She marches over and punches me in the shoulder, the one that I bashed into a rock in the Colorado. I go down to my knees in agony.

"Christ! That's the shoulder I hurt."

"Serves you right!"

I make a mental note on the right ways and the wrong ways to tease Dallas. Tossing what looks like a realistic suicide vest at her is definitely the wrong way.

The trunk of the Focus has all the excess supplies I used to create the vest, the dead man's switch, and the fake bag of dynamite I gave to Mr. Short and Stocky. We transfer it all over to the crew cab of the truck.

I brief her on the details of that bluff as we work.

"Talia is looking dumber and dumber," Dallas says. "She should have just put a bullet in your head. And you did all this after knowing June a day?"

"Yeah."

"Before you were in love?"

I shrug. "I got us into that mess. Besides, I think I kinda always was."

I'm moving stuff and Dallas is standing there, dimly illuminated by my flashlight and the cab light of the truck, her hands on her hips.

"What?" I ask, a half-full bag of sand—what the faux dynamite is filled with—in my arms.

She walks up to me, takes my cheeks in her hands, and kisses me straight on the lips. It's not a romantic kiss, she kept her mouth closed and it is only brief.

"What was that for?" I ask.

"Being a decent human being in a world gone mad."

Now I'm staring at her, blinking. Yeah, rescuing June was the right thing to do, but I'm still full of angst about what happened in Phoenix, and the two feelings are at war.

She takes the sand from me, throws it in the truck, and asks, "What's next?"

JUST WEST OF US, I-40 crosses Padre Canyon, a separate bridge for each direction. The west-bound bridge had been recently rebuilt and there's some construction equipment there, a small trailer, and one of those metal shipping containers.

During my bluff with Mr. Short and Stocky, when he demanded that I produce dynamite or he would hurt June, I made a show of driving out here in case they were watching. I did search, but not very well. My bluff was already underway, and I did not want to, under any circumstances, give that psychotic ass any real dynamite. Besides, I didn't have the time.

It's a long shot and we need some shelter anyway, so with the sun just starting to come up, we park the truck behind the trailer and out of view of Mount Elden, and Dallas and I search a second time.

The trailer is useless, but the shipping container is a god-awful mess. It's like when the world went mad, they just threw everything in here. Hand tools, orange cones, construction signs, some jerry cans with gasoline—those go in the truck—, surveying equipment, and some things I just can't identify.

As the sun comes up and the container heats up, we slowly sift through the crap, moving much of it out of the container. We're lucky in that the open end is shielded from Elden by the trailer and we can work quickly.

A few hours later, we get to the back and we find a metal box the size of a small foot locker. I bust the lock and in it, sealed in plastic bags, are stick after stick of dynamite. Plus, a smaller box with several types of blasting caps, wire, and fuse.

Dallas's whoop echoes in the enclosed space and she slaps me on the back. She runs out of the container, points herself north, and screams, "We're coming to blow you up, Talia. You hear that, you sociopathic bitch!"

I pull out one bag and carefully bring it into the light, holding it like a newborn baby, careful not to jostle it. When I get a good look at it, I swear.

"What!?" Dallas asks.

I point inside the sealed plastic at a few crystals that have formed near one end of the dynamite.

Dallas shrugs.

"That's nitroglycerin. The dynamite is old, it's sweating, it's very volatile at this point."

"Volatile?"

I nod. "This little baby gets dropped and then..."

"Boom?" she asks.

I nod. "Boom!"

She's wide-eyed and blinking at me. "June's worth it," she says. Her voice is weak and it comes out as half question.

I smile. "She is." I'm scared, but I have no doubt that June Medina is worth it.

CHAPTER FOUR

I SPEND the next hour in the shipping container having banished Dallas to the trailer to get some rest. She said she was too nervous, so I showed her how to make the fake dynamite. We are going to need more of it.

I'm not worried about Zs out here that much, although Twin Arrows Casino is not far away and there are likely a bunch there, but it's well beyond zombie radar range. I'm not too worried about Mr. Short and Stocky and his gang either—there's no reason for them to come out this way.

What I am worried about is an explosion.

I tried to get Dallas to go across the highway to the ancient trading post, but her answer was her middle finger. Having spent a few days with her, it's quite clear that it's her favorite finger and she enjoys using it whenever she can.

The trailer is a compromise. I've got one door to the storage container shut and while the blast, if it happens, will direct some energy towards the trailer, I'm hoping it will be mostly contained.

Well... I'm hoping I don't blow myself up. Really, I am.

One stick at a time, I pull the dynamite out. I'm using a flashlight

—it's fairly dark back there—and examine them. I am relieved to find that not all of the sticks have sweat an equal amount. Some have almost no nitroglycerin crystals. A few have none.

My heart is beating hard the whole time, sweat dripping into my eyes, my hands slick from the sweat.

But I go slow. I keep rubbing my hands on a towel. I go through one stick at a time, getting the best ones.

I put the good ones back in the box, pack rags around them, and carefully carry it to the truck, put it on the seat of the crew cab, and buckle it in.

"What's next?" Dallas asks. She looks strung out, I'm sure she didn't even try to close her eyes. I know I wouldn't have been able to rest.

"We create a little more faux dynamite and then we sleep. We can't do anything else until dark."

She nods.

"And after that, we rig the rest of the dynamite to blow if someone comes sniffing around."

Her eyes go wide, but there is no Dallas-like whoop. I guess explosives are a bit over her limit. I am relieved to find that the wild Lonestar has a limit.

CHAPTER FIVE

AFTER DARK, as we pull away, the shipping container has a couple of sentences scratched on the metal: "Dangerous explosives inside! This will go off if you open the door." Below that, scrawled by Dallas, it says, "Seriously! Walk away now or die, dummy!" And then she drew the image of a hand with the middle finger raised.

The rigging is simple, really. The remaining dynamite is in a cardboard box up high on a shelf with a string tied to the second door of the shipping container. Opening it will pull the box down and the odds of the nitro igniting are high.

No one will see it unless they go through this site, but with the dynamite just getting more dangerous with time, I wanted to both warn and try to keep it out of the hands of dummies.

And, yeah, I'm the one cruising down I-40 with my headlights off as dusk slides into darkness with a container full of dynamite. But hey, I'm trying to save the woman of my post-apocalyptic dreams, so maybe I'm more of a fool in love than a dummy.

I glance over at Dallas and she gives me a weak smile. Even with her around, I think laughter is going to be hard to come by today.

We go "shopping" at Best Buy, OfficeMax, and Home Depot and

find what we need. Again, we're lucky. I even snag a few journals and some good pens so I can start writing for real. It's on our way out of town that our luck runs out.

We're just heading out on 89 going north, back towards Cameron and the Grand Canyon. There's a quicker way to get to the Grand Canyon Village on the South Rim, but I don't dare try to drive all the way through Flagstaff. There's another gang at the university.

We've just passed Townsend-Winona Road and all the wrecks and blockages are behind us. I'm picking up speed when a pickup truck lurches into the road and blocks both lanes, men in the bed pointing rifles at us.

I throw the truck into reverse and another truck blocks our way back with more men and more rifles.

There are four lanes here and soon all of them are blocked by trucks, lights shining on us, guns pointed at us. The psychotic, petty, wannabe warlord found us. It has to be him.

Dallas curses with gusto and then adds, "What do we do now?"

I could head off the road, go around them, but there is no getting away from that many trucks and that many guns.

"Stall them," I hiss, "but don't leave the truck. And find out what Mr. Short and Stocky's real name is."

I pull the suicide vest out from the crew cab and put it on. I then crawl over the seat, into the back, and dig into the dynamite case.

"Hey, officers!" Dallas calls in a cheerful voice. She opens the door and stands in behind it. "Were we going too fast? We kinda thought that with the apocalypse and all that no one cared anymore."

I'm moving as fast as I can with the dynamite, but I really can't go that fast.

"Where is he?" a male voice shouts from the trucks in front of us. I can't see him, but I recognize his voice. Mr. Short and Stocky. "Diamondback and I need to have a discussion."

Dallas sticks her head into the cab and says, "'Diamondback,' ha! He thinks of you as Diamondback. That, my friend, is your new nickname... for however long we live."

"Just stall," I hiss, my hands shaking from the 5-hour energy drinks we both slammed before hitting the road.

"Yeah, Diamondback will be right with you," Dallas calls. "But in the meantime, maybe you can settle a little debate for us. Seeing as you guys were never properly introduced, Diamondback refers to you as 'Mr. Short and Stocky.' Me, personally, I find that a bit ironic given that Diamondback himself is fairly short and fairly stocky."

I have a stick of dynamite out of its plastic wrapper and am inserting a safety fuse into the thin metal blasting cap, my hands shaking, my breath coming fast, the mountain night suddenly hot. I crimp the end of the blasting cap with my multi-tool so the fuse won't come out.

"I mean," Dallas continues, "short and stocky works for me, provided the man is kind, has a heart, you know?"

"What are you talking about?" Mr. Short and Stocky yells. I figure we're still alive because he wants to kill me personally, and up close.

"Oh. Sorry," she replies. "Please forgive me. Not that many people to have conversations with these days. Let me get to the point. Your name. Diamondback thinks of you as Mr. Short and Stocky, but another friend of mine just thinks of you as Asshole. I'm wondering what your real name is, so when we have a conversation about you, we can use the correct moniker."

I cringe and push the completed blasting cap and fuse into the dynamite. Dallas is doing her thing, crossing every line possible. I expect the bullets to fly at any moment.

I hear a chuckle. "Asshole. I like that. Was that what the skinny girl called me?"

"Yes, sir, Mr. Asshole."

"You are not so skinny of a girl," he says. "I like that, maybe I won't kill you. So, get your friend out here. Now!"

"But your name," Dallas says, her voice taking on a girlish whine. "Please."

He sighs. "Brown. Call me Mr. Brown."

Dallas ducks her head back in the cab. "God, that's a boring name. You ready yet?"

I nod and step out of the truck, suicide vest on, one hand held high with the dead man's switch, the other holding the stick of dynamite.

Mr. Brown laughs, it's loud, kind of this overdone guffaw, and very appropriate for a psychotic, petty, wannabe warlord, but it doesn't last long. "I won't fall for that two times, boy."

I nod. "If you don't mind, I thought we might have a quick demonstration before you kill me."

He shrugs. "Sure. Your friend has put me in a good mood and I am feeling generous."

"How did you find us?" I ask.

He points out in the darkness back towards Flagstaff. "We have someone on top of the tower of the pet food factory now."

I nod. It makes sense, it's the highest thing besides the mountain in the area. He's extended his territory while I was gone.

"I have a deal for you," I say, wiggling the stick of dynamite. "After our last meeting, I've made it my mission to find real dynamite. I've been all over the area. I know where it all is now."

"Bullshit." He spits the word out and I get the feeling he wants to spit on me... for starters. My bluff must have shamed him, and that's really the last thing you want to do to a psychotic, petty, wannabe warlord.

My hands are high as I walk forward a few steps until I'm halfway between our truck and his. The night is cool and all gloomy darkness except for the harsh pool of light created by the headlights.

I carefully set down the stick and slowly step back.

"It's real," I say. "That's about a ten-second fuse. Light it, but I suggest you throw it far."

Brown nods at one of his beefy boys who recovers the dynamite and returns.

"Real, you say?" he calls.

"Yes. Real. No bullshit."

"And your deal?"

"We just raided a store not far from here. I couldn't take it all. You let us go, I'll tell you where to find the dynamite."

He's silent as he fingers the stick of dynamite and I can almost see the wheels moving in his head. He holds the stick to his face and sniffs, his brow furrowing below his brown-grey buzzed hair.

"I must tell you," I say, "that I found C4 as well as dynamite and my employer has it all except for this. She knows where we are, she knows when to expect us. She knows about you. If I don't make it back with this she'll come looking, and believe me, you won't like that."

He's holding the dynamite and starts pacing back and forth in front of the trucks.

"Lies. All lies," he says.

"Light it," I say, slowly stepping back to the truck. "See if I'm lying."

"What have you got to lose, Mr. Asshole?" Dallas shouts. And then quieter to me, but loud enough for them to hear. "I don't think he's got the balls or the sense. Isn't it better to get some dynamite than to start a war?"

I suppress a smile. There are no women among Mr. Brown's group, and having a woman suggest he's lacking balls is perfect. I don't know him well, but in many ways, I think he's worse than Talia.

Someone pulls out a lighter and I duck behind the open door to the truck and yell, "Throw it as far as you can."

The fuse hisses to life and Brown throws it into the trees on the side of the road. He's got a good arm, but the stick hits a tree and falls to the ground. I dive into the truck and Dallas does the same.

There is a bright flash of light and the truck is buffeted right before the sound of the explosion smashes into my ears. A few moments later dirt and pine needles come raining down.

There are curses and whoops and hollers, the loudest, of course, from Dallas who's slapping me on the back. "Oh my God, Woody.

Holy Shit! I want to shove one of those bad boys up Talia's ass and light up. Whoop!"

Silence descends as the shock and adrenaline wear off and Brown and his gang start thinking about the implications of dynamite and what it means and what they can do with it.

"Now get out there and sell it, Diamondback," Dallas hisses and shoves me towards to door.

I walk out, the dead man's switch held high. "Do we have a deal?" I shout. The air has an acrid, smoky smell to it and there is some mumbling from the trucks both in front of and behind us.

"You expect me to trust you?" Brown asks.

"Kill me or trust me," I say. "Take a chance on acquiring dynamite or start a war you will lose." I shrug as casually as I can but am shaking inside from the caffeine and adrenaline.

Mr. Brown stares at me for the longest time before nodding his head.

CHAPTER SIX

"I MEAN, the fools are going to get there and probably blow themselves up," Dallas says, the energy in her voice just making me feel exhausted.

I told Brown where to get the dynamite, out at Padre Canyon, even explained that I was so rushed the first time I was there, I couldn't really search properly.

She's driving and I'm in the back rigging more sticks of dynamite and working on the suicide vest. We're past the turnoff to Sunset Crater, 89A making its quick decent down into the desert, the pine trees shrinking to be replaced by juniper trees and then the grasses of the high desert.

"We can hope," I say, quietly.

My mind is spinning. Brown is mean, and fairly smart, but Talia is smarter and with more at stake.

"I mean, what a brilliant combination of the truth and BS. Diamondback strikes again!"

"You know, I don't think I like that nickname."

"Too damn bad, Diamondback. You rattle and the petty, mean... wait, what is your phrase?"

"Psychotic, petty, wannabe warlords."

"Yeah, you rattle and the psychotic, petty, wannabe warlords go-a-runnin'!"

We hit a bump and I almost drop the stick of dynamite I'm holding. Probably nothing would have happened, but my heart does a tap dance in my chest.

"Slow down there, Lonestar. I'm handling dynamite back here. Besides, I've got a lot to do before we meet Talia."

"Sure. Sure. Man, I feel alive. Do you feel alive, Diamondback?"

"Yeah. I feel super alive," I say dryly. "Now, please slow down so we *stay* alive."

ᛤᛤ ᛏᛏ ᛤᛤ

WE MAKE it to Desert View without incident and head west twenty-five miles, paralleling the rim of the Grand Canyon to Grand Canyon Village. This is where all the tourists came, and this is where that zombie herd must have originated before it took to wandering along the rim in search of living flesh and delicious brains.

My theory—and you knew I had one, didn't you?—is that the herd started at the Grand Canyon Village and cleaned the area out, either eating or chasing away all the living humans, not to mention the animals.

And then they got hungry, but there were a lot of them, so their fungal super brain (remember their fresh meat radar was much better in a group) had the bright idea of trying different territory, so they probably wandered west all the way out to Hermit's Rest and then back east all the way to Desert View.

From time to time as they wandered back and forth, they'd come across new groups of the living who figured the Grand Canyon might be a good place to hole up, or trap animals that hadn't long since vacated the area.

They found enough food this way so that their wanderings became something of a regular patrol.

Okay, end of theory, back to the rescue.

We don't stop, we drive right to Bright Angel Lodge, park in front, and get on Bright Angel Trail and start the ten-mile hike down to Phantom Ranch.

It's been four days since we left June with Talia and I'm worried. Worried how Talia has treated her, hoping she is still alive. I'm worried about this plan that June and I sketched out in our three days in the forest on the North Rim. Will it work? Is there even a shot?

In one respect, I am grateful for the encounter with Brown and company. It was kind of like a dress rehearsal and gave me a few more ideas.

Our packs are loaded down and very heavy. We've got the altered suicide vest, water, food, and electronics. Plus, I'm carrying the bag of fake and real dynamite. I have every portable solar charger we could find hanging off my pack to charge the batteries we need. We might actually have to delay a day, so we have enough sunshine to charge them.

"So, what do you think our odds are?" Dallas asks as we start down the switchbacks, lighting our way with a flashlight. It's a few hours until dawn.

"Of what?" I ask. "Saving June or finishing Talia?"

"Let's start with Talia."

"Oh, those odds are good. As long we get her onto the bridge, she's likely going down one way or another."

"And saving June?" she asks quietly. "And all of us hiking back out?"

I shake my head. "Not so good."

We're quiet for a long time and then I add, "But you, Lonestar, your odds of survival are quite good. You're our sniper so you won't be in the thick of it."

She's unusually silent and angst is almost radiating off her.

"Naw," she says. "If my new best friend doesn't make it, well... let's just say I could get a little crazy."

I open my mouth to argue with her, but who am I to tell anyone how to live in this post-A world. Hell, I'm hiking, caring a bag full of explosives and a suicide vest that isn't quite fake anymore. Who am I to tell Dallas how to live much less die?

"You want to talk that part through?" I finally ask. "I mean if you're going to go 'a little crazy,' you might as well be smart about it."

She sniffs and rubs at her face but doesn't speak right away. "Yeah, that... that'd be great."

So we spend the next few miles talking about how if June and I don't make it, Dallas will ensure that Talia and a few of the crueler members of Phantom Company don't make it either. We even allocate a few sticks of dynamite to the "Lonestar Goes Berserk" plan.

Morbid? Yes. But if the apocalypse did anything, it opened our eyes to the gift of life and the inevitability of death. Best live the former as well as you can before that latter comes calling.

CHAPTER SEVEN

PLANS like these are hard to make. They don't descend fully formed from the heavens. Getting boots on the ground can change every-thing, and having someone more familiar with the surroundings can help.

Dallas and I talk it through on the hike down. We talk sporadi-cally and quietly, keeping our ears open for Zs. We take breaks frequently because of our heavy loads.

So, my first idea was to get Talia and company on the Kaibab Suspension Bridge, but that won't work. Dallas reminds me that the sides are metal railings about five feet high. The same is true for the Bright Angel Bridge, making them both a bad place for the exchange. I need Dallas to have a clear shot.

"If Talia actually goes for trading June for dynamite, June is gonna..." Dallas let out a long, low whistle. "Well, let's just say that hell hath no fury like a military trained woman traded for explosives."

I chuckle, grateful for anything resembling laughter. I can't imagine June being happy to be traded for explosives, but I'm sure she'll be glad to be out of there. But that isn't all the trade is about.

We will rain holy hell down on them if Talia doesn't give us June, so there is that.

We switch the trade location to right across the Bright Angel Bridge. We need them in the open and I want Talia to bring lots of her people. Their numbers don't increase our danger and I have a hunch it will help. Well, a hope at least, that June has made some headway down there.

The sun comes up as we descend, and as much as I hate to do it, we stop before the final descent into the inner gorge—where we would be visible to Phantom Company—and hike off the trail a good ways and find shelter.

We spend the day alternating between sleep and prep—there are still some electronics to rig, batteries to charge, and a note to write to Talia.

While Dallas sleeps, I pull my "Woody and June versus the Apocalypse" notes out and scribble down more details. I've got one of the journals we picked up at OfficeMax and I just start to write more notes and then start writing it as a story. I feel this pressure, the need to... well, it's kind of confessing my sins, I guess, but I know I'm a long way from writing about Phoenix, so I start in Flagstaff at the dog food plant, because shouldn't a love story start when the couple meets?

And I am hoping that this is a love story, one with a happy ending.

Really, I need this love story to have a happy ending, despite the apocalypse, despite the prevalence of zombies and psychotic, petty, wannabe warlords. I feel it in my stomach, which is a tight knot, and I'm hungry and nauseous at the same time.

But writing helps, so I give in to the pressure to write, and I write, as fast as I can.

I don't stop to think about that pressure then, but with just a little hindsight, it's clear that I don't believe that we will succeed, that we will survive this rescue attempt, and I need to capture something of Woody and June that will outlive us.

The words just pour out of me and I write as quickly as I can. I focus on remembering our words as clearly as possible, the sights and smells of our journey, how things felt—all the things that will quickly fade from memory.

When Dallas stirs, I stow the journal back in my pack, not ready to talk about what I'm doing, and certainly not ready for a biting comment from her.

I go back to rigging the dead man's switch, making it real this time.

"How'd you learn to do all that?" Dallas asks sleepily as she pushes herself up into a sitting position, yawns and stretches.

"It's not complicated," I say, holding up the jury-rigged assembly. It's the hacked off handle of a leaf blower, red electrical tape over the spring-loaded switch with wires dangling from it. There's a couple of LEDs embedded in the bottom of a handle that glow red when it's powered. "It's a switch, altered to be off when pressed and on when released, some LEDs just for show, some wires, a battery, and an electronic detonator."

"Blasting cap?" she asks

I nod. "The detonator. Some of the blasting caps use a fuse, some can be triggered electronically."

"So... how'd you learn all this crap?"

I nod vaguely to the south. "All post-A. I was in that group in northern Phoenix led by one of those charismatic psychopaths."

"Wait," she says, holding her hand up. "I'll get it this time." She sits up straight, her face serious. "Petty, pustulant, pouty, psychotic, pedantic person..."

I just sit there shaking my head. "No."

"Hmmm... Let me try again. Psychotic, always-gotta-be-right, power-hungry, post-apocalyptic asshole?"

I crack a smile. "I like that one."

"So... he was one of those?"

"Oh yeah, makes Talia look like a kindergarten teacher. He had an old dude working for him he called 'Q,' à la James Bond, and the guy took a shine to me and taught me all this stuff. Taught me about electronics and explosives and lots of crazy things."

Dallas is quiet for a while, drinks some water, and we share a very stale power bar. "What happened to Q?"

I shake my head. "You don't want to hear my confession, remember?"

Dallas nods. We've all seen the bad side of the apocalypse, and in some ways, we are living it now. But it's different this time, right? I've got purpose and friends, people who aren't psychopaths or petty, and have no desire to be warlords. I can let go of the past, right?

"He's gone," I add, feeling the weight of it bearing down on me again.

"So you're Q now," she says, scooting over the dirt and sitting next to me. "Show me."

Her face is hard to read, maybe she wants to know, maybe she's just trying to distract me—in either case, I can use the distraction. I show her each piece of the dead man's switch, all the changes I made, put in the battery, and feel the electricity when the switch is released. We then get some longer wire, hook up a blasting cap, and make sure it works.

It does. Once I add real dynamite to the suicide vest, I can officially blow myself up.

Now I've got something that in one fell swoop violates both of my rules for each day. First, it will kill me, so survival is out; and second, having real dynamite and a real dead man's switch is going to make it extraordinarily hard to laugh.

And my newly minted third rule of spending time with June... well, that's what this is all about.

CHAPTER EIGHT

WE SNEAK down the rest of the way during dusk, when it's light enough for us to see the trail without flashlights, and dark enough so that it will be hard for the Phantom Company sentries to see us.

Dallas assures me that odds are low. She was a sentry, and besides guarding the bridges, they were supposed to watch the trails on the other side, but in reality, they all get bored and don't do nearly enough of that.

Bright Angel Trail ends at the suspension bridge and River Trail connects to Kaibab Trail and that suspension bridge. Much of River Trail is exposed and in clear view of the sentries.

We can't bushwhack around, the terrain is just too rugged, the cliff of the inner gorge too steep, so we have to use the trail.

Once in sight of the river, we stop until it's nearly pitch dark and move slowly and carefully on the trail past the Bright Angel bridge.

My heart is pounding and I can barely breath. The noise of the rushing river will overwhelm any noise we might make, but they could spot us.

We go slow and steady, in case anyone is looking over this way, so they don't catch any movement in the darkness. We get past the bridge and go up River Trail, which is mostly carved into the side of the cliff and the 1.5-billion-year-old Vishnu Schist.

I think of my old friend Q, his grey hair and wrinkled face, his Boston accent. If this was his territory, he'd have rigged solar-powered motion sensors and what Dallas and I are doing would be impossible. Alarms would be going off by now.

Just because there's been an apocalypse, doesn't mean you have to completely abandon knowledge and technology... not to mention civility and compassion.

Once we get up River Trail a ways, we find a perfect spot for Dallas right off the trail. Perfect in the sense that you can see both bridges and all of the Bright Angel Creek delta that Phantom Company is farming and housing their burros on.

What's not perfect is it's right off the trail and quite exposed. But we don't really have a choice. Dallas tells me this trail gets patrolled every few days, but isn't actually used. If a patrol comes out, we'll see them, but our campaign to get June back starts at first light, so hopefully there won't be any patrols.

We settle in behind a large boulder and try to rest, but I find it impossible. There are too many things that can go wrong. Too many ways to die. And way too few ways for this to work.

CHAPTER NINE

BEFORE DAWN, I pack up my gear. I need to be closer to the bridge.

"You got this, Diamondback," Dallas says, tugging at my ball cap.

I nod, too nervous to even speak. Success means June, failure means death. I don't see how the stakes can get higher.

"And if you don't..." I see her shrug in starlit darkness. "Well, Talia will have to deal with Lonestar armed with a hunting rifle and not a goddamn thing to lose."

I swallow hard. "I'll do my best so that doesn't have to happen."

We're silent and I hear Dallas sniff. "Get June back, okay? I was awful to you two and want to have a chance to make it up to her."

"Yeah. I'll get her back." I try to sound confident, but am anything but.

She pulls me into a hug and holds me tight and I hug her back. She sniffs more and so do I.

"You are not to shoot unless this goes south, right?" I say.

"Yes, Woody. No shooting."

"And 'goes south' means June and I are already dead. Nothing short of that. Nothing. Do you hear me?"

She lets go of me. "I got it, Woody, I do. If you and June live, Talia lives."

I stare at her, not that I can really see her face with the sky to the east just starting to lighten. I need this mission to be more important than her vengeance. Can I trust her?

I take her hand and squeeze it, my hand shaking.

"I won't let you down," she whispers and then kisses me on the cheek.

I let go and make my slow way down the exposed trail, past the bridge, and take cover behind a mesquite tree right off the trail. It's terrible cover, as these things go, but I won't need it long.

In the dark, I get a drone out, a high-end quadcopter with HD camera and about twenty minutes of run time. I attach a live piece of dynamite, with blasting cap and fuse, and attach the white flag and note we wrote. I power up the tablet and attach it to the drone controller, which is basically two little joysticks, two antennas, and a few buttons.

My hands are shaking, and I have to slow myself down. I whisper to myself, just like I did when Dallas and I walked away from June, "This is not over, this is not over, this is *not* over."

Please don't let this be over.

By some miracle, I've found a reason to live in this world and I so want to live now. Not just survive, but *live*.

As soon as there's enough light for the drone's camera to work, I get my binoculars out and look for June's sign. We had planned this when we were being hunted by Phantom Company. I search frantically in the dim light trying to find it.

If I don't find it, June and I agreed that I would abort any rescue attempt because it would mean she wasn't alive.

Five minutes of searching, and I don't see it and I decide to join Lonestar in her berserker plan, shed my humanity, and embrace the apocalypse.

But, no, there it is. In the rocks on the hill above the burro stables are five sticks sticking up in the gravelly dirt next to three rocks forming a small cairn. June survived five days. This is day six since we parted.

She's okay.

I wipe the sweat from my brow and launch the drone, sending it up river several hundred yards, across the Colorado, and downstream as fast as it will go.

I stop it just past the bridge, the camera trained on the sentries, two thirty-something men. I recognize them from our time with Phantom Company, but don't know their names.

Their jaws fall open, which makes me smile, the sign must be working, because they don't shoot the drone. The top of the sign says, "Live Dynamite Attached. Do Not Shoot Unless You Want to DIE!"

Right below it says, "Will trade dynamite for June. Get Talia now! Cross either bridge and you die, both are rigged to explode."

In smaller text are more instructions on the exchange and on testing the dynamite. I land the drone and one of the sentries goes running.

This is it. Showtime.

CHAPTER TEN

AN HOUR LATER, right after I puke what little I have in my stomach, I put on the suicide vest, put my green army surplus jacket on over it, attach the dead man's switch with the button firmly pressed down, and zip up the jacket.

I am now a bomb.

My heart pounds hard and I feel dizzy, standing there for a moment until I can get myself under control. I take a deep breath, pick up the bag of dynamite, and make my way onto the trail and walk onto the Bright Angel Suspension Bridge.

The drone's batteries died before Talia got back, but they have tested the dynamite attached to the drone and followed the instructions.

At the bridge, I put down the bag and use my binoculars, one-handed of course, and see the group approaching. Talia in the lead, with Harris, Sal, and Mary. I only see a glimpse of June's black hair, she's shorter than the rest of them and in the middle of the group.

I look towards where I know Dallas is and do my best to smile. I don't feel like a diamondback rattlesnake. I feel like a boy who has gotten way in over his head and wishes the adults would swoop in and straighten it all out.

With the jacket and the nerves, I am sweating profusely despite the cool morning.

This bridge has a series of gates set up, just like the Kaibab Bridge, that are easy for the living to open and walk through. I leave them all open.

I get a glimpse of June as I get towards the other side of the bridge. Her face doesn't look right. I stop and use my binoculars. She has a cracked lip and her left cheek is swollen. I grip the dead man's switch so hard that my sweaty fingers are in danger of slipping off.

Then I see Talia and smile. The tall woman has one eye nearly swollen shut. Whatever happened, it appears both of them took a few good blows. I hope I live long enough to hear the story.

The gate on the far side is tall with razor wire on the top and locked. There is one terrified-looking guard there who opens the gate for me.

"Back with them," I say, nodding towards the group standing just a few yards back from the gate.

He nods and seems happy to be getting away from me.

"Hello, Talia," I say as I approach, getting a better look at her bruised face. I can just imagine Dallas smiling ear-to-ear seeing this through her rifle scope. "Have a bad spill or something?"

Her lips purse, and she raises one thin eyebrow, but she doesn't say anything.

"You okay, June?" I ask.

"Just fine," she says, her tone tight.

"Let's see it," Talia says.

I walk forward a few steps, drop the bag of dynamite, and back up. There is a blinking LED taped to it with some wires running into the bag, very similar to the pack I gave Mr. Short and Stocky up on Mount Elden.

Talia nods to Sal, who walks slowly up to the bag.

"Unzip it," I say. "Feel free to look, but don't touch any of the wires."

Sal whistles and then says, "Shit! There are a bunch a nails in here with the dynamite."

"Insurance," I say.

"What the hell are you talking about?" Talia asks.

I slowly unzip my jacket with my free hand and reveal the suicide vest, which is covered in sticks of dynamite with nails glued to them. I push my left hand out of the sleeve of my jacket and show them the dead man's switch. "The detonator blows both. If the blast doesn't do the job, the nails will."

Jaws drop and there are gasps. I smile, feeling less nervous now that the confrontation is finally here.

"So there's the dynamite," I say. "June and I will be going now."

Talia doesn't move, her one good eye boring into me. I'm not expecting this to be easy, but I'm not prepared for what she does next.

She steps forward boldly, kicks the bag of dynamite aside and walks right up to me. She's several inches taller than me and I have to look up to meet her eyes.

"Bullshit!" she says. "You wouldn't kill your precious June, you doe-eyed weakling."

She pulls a knife out so quick I can't react and pokes several of the sticks on my suicide vest. They start leaking sand, and before I can say a thing, the knife is back on her belt and her gun is pressed to my forehead, pushing the brim of my hat up. "Any last words, Woody Woodpecker? Because, ttthattt's all, folks."

I blink, my mind still catching up with her boldness. "You're wrong. Some of the dynamite is fake, I'll give you that, but some is real." My heart is pounding and I am sweating all over, drops sliding into my eyes and stinging.

"Bullshit!"

"You haven't pulled the trigger, so you can't be sure, so let me prove it."

The gun leaves my forehead and she backs up a step.

"I am prepared to die today, so is June. We had plenty of time to talk about this out in the forest."

Talia twists around and glances at June's crossed arms, pursed lips, and hard eyes.

With my free hand, I point at a cluster of sticks over my sternum. "Look closely. See those small crystals. These sticks are old, they're sweating. That is nitroglycerin. The bag has fake sticks, but four real ones too, and lots of screws and nails."

Talia's jaw is moving, her cheeks flushing red, I can see the fury in her eyes.

"The first time I did this, it was a bluff, but not this time. I found dynamite, you already proved it. Do you somehow think I only found one stick?"

Talia is breathing heavily and her whole face is red now, she steps back up to me and presses the gun to my forehead. "I don't believe you. Maybe some of the dynamite is real, you wouldn't kill yourself, you wouldn't kill *her*."

"Just because you've never had anyone you'd be willing to die for, doesn't mean I don't."

My mind flashes to Dallas, I can see her, her finger tensing on the trigger, sweat beading her brow, her heart beating fast, wanting to kill Talia, but trying to hold back. I just hope our bond is strong enough, because if Talia dies, June and I are dead... for sure.

And somehow that empowers me, and I feel this growing boldness. I'm going to die, either Dallas will lose it or Talia will shoot. What is there to lose?

"Go ahead, Talia," I say, my voice getting stronger. "Shoot. Kill us all. End this now. Do it!"

Seconds tick by and I can't see her well with the gun to my forehead, but she is getting even redder. "Okay," she says calmly, slowly pulling back the hammer.

Time slows down all cliched, B-movie style, and I can hear each heartbeat reverberating through my brain, each breath flowing past my nose, down into my lungs. The essence of life, heart and breath, becoming so loud right before they are about to be extinguished.

The psychotic part of Talia was the one thing we couldn't predict. What path the pressure of our attack would push her down, whether she would choose death rather than defeat.

And in her mind, there is a chance I'm bluffing with the dead man's switch, that the wires don't actually do anything. She's partially right, the bag is a bluff, I didn't have the right equipment to do a wireless trigger, but the vest is not.

She shoots, we all die.

I hear shouts and see a flash of movement. June breaks free of the others, surges forward, and dives towards Talia.

It's not going to work, she's going to fall short.

The beating of my heart grows louder in my head and my breath seems to slow.

Talia slowly squeezes the trigger.

I love you, June Medina.

You better, Woody Beckman!

June's dive turns into a roll just as the hammer starts to fall. I feel a surprising moment of peace there between the heartbeats, between the breaths, when I'm still alive but everything is still. I love June and she knows it. I found love in this completely insane world. While I do want more time, isn't that really what it's all about?

As the hammer is about to hit the back of the bullet, June's feet slam into the back of Talia's knees and the gun flies up right as the bullet fires, knocking my hat off, parting my hair, scraping my skull, but not blowing my brains out.

And then time falls back on me with more force than the Colorado when I was thrown into that rapid. I fall to my knees holding the dead man switch tight, clamping my second hand over the first, my ears ringing from the gunshot.

Blood is oozing from the wound, trickling down my forehead, the bullet's trail burning, but I ignore it.

Talia scrambles to her feet cursing, there are shouts from Sal and Harris and Mary, but I can't hear them.

June is there, her face just inches from me and I inhale deeply of her sweet and sweaty scent, her blue eyes locking with mine.

"I love you, Woody Beckman," she says.

My heart skips a beat. She's saying that because she thinks we're all about to die.

"You better, June Medina."

CHAPTER ELEVEN

THERE'S SHOUTING AND CURSING, a huge argument is going on around us, but I try to suck up as much of the ocean blue eyes of June as I can. I try to breathe her in, memorize her face, feel her breath.

"She shot you," June says, her tone even.

I nod, I can feel the slow trickle of blood on my forehead and a fiery burn where the bullet grazed me. "Just a flesh wound," I say.

"The vest is real, right?" she asks.

I nod. "And Dallas has Talia in her scope right now."

"Okay. I have a *plan*." She ends with a wicked smile, but before I can say anything she slowly stands up and brushes off her jeans.

The argument is fierce and seems to come down to whether Talia almost got them all killed. It's Talia and Sal against Harris and Mary.

"We're just going to leave now," June says quietly, "and let you all sort this out. Seems like a family affair to me."

Somehow, her voice filters through the noise and they all stop and then four guns are pointed at us.

"I don't think so," Talia says.

June ignores her. "Harris, Mary, Sal, listen to me. We talked about this. How much effort and how much risk did Talia expend to get me back? How many of you could I have killed when you captured me? I don't want to be here, Talia knows this. She did this just to have what she wants, to prove that she is right.

"Every deal she's made with us was either an outright lie, or stacked so survival was nearly impossible."

"Shut up, June," Talia says, walking to June and aiming the gun at her head. "I will only warn you once."

"Woody's vest is real. Under Talia's leadership, we will all die. If I hadn't stopped her we would already be dead."

Talia's face is beet red again and I know that June has gone too far. She has crossed the line with Talia and is now the enemy.

Talia cocks her gun, but Harris slides behind her and presses his gun to her back. "Now, now," he says, his jaw bunching. "I want to hear what the young lady has to say."

"Ask yourself," June continues, "are Woody and I worth this war? We didn't want to stay, if we had just been given the option to leave, none of this would have happened." She locks eyes with Harris. "Make no mistake, we either walk away, or people die."

I slowly get to my feet, feeling as weak as a rag doll, and pull a handkerchief from my pocket and wipe the blood out of my face. "There are four real pieces of dynamite in that bag, with blasting caps and a few feet of safety fuse," I say. "My offer was an honest one. But the sticks are old and must be handled with care. We're lucky they didn't blow when she kicked the bag. Yet another brilliant decision on the part of your leader."

Now Sal's gun is pointed at Talia and Mary's too.

"You've got a good thing going here, Tal," June says, gesturing up the canyon towards Phantom Ranch. "But I think it's time for a council, not a petty dictator."

June walks up to me takes my free hand and we walk towards the bridge. I let go of June long enough to pick up my Arizona Diamondback's hat. It has a bullet hole where the bill joins with the hat. I smile and put it back on by bloody head.

"As soon as you are at a safe distance," Talia yells, her voice high-pitched and hysterical, "I'm going to get a rifle and kill you both!"

June turns. "Harris, Sal, Mary, do we have a deal? The dynamite for our safe release, no pursuit?"

"Yes," Harris says.

"I don't care what they say!" Talia snarls. "I'll leave. I'll hunt you down myself. I'll see you both dead."

"I should mention," June adds, "that Dallas has you in her sites right now. She's itching for some payback. Shall I have Woody give her the signal?"

"And I mean," I add, "it took everything I had to convince her not to kill you on sight." I look around the open Bright Angel Creek delta. "And you guys might want to think more about security. You aren't nearly as safe here as you think."

Talia opens her mouth to shout more threats, but Harris hits her on the head with the butt of his gun and she goes down in a heap.

"Can you restrain her for a couple of days? Give us time to regroup and get out of the area?" June asks.

Sal chuckles. "That would be a distinct pleasure."

Just because I can't stand it anymore, I disable the dead man's switch by slowly disconnecting the wires. I'm suddenly panting harder now that the danger of immediate death is past. We can either trust them or we can't, so now or later doesn't make a big difference. I give a thumbs-up signal in Dallas's direction to let her know we're good.

I take June's hand and squeeze it, her eyes bright, her smile wide, and we walk across the bridge towards our future... together.

CHAPTER TWELVE

TO SAY our reunion with Dallas is enthusiastic is like saying the sun is hot. It doesn't cover it, not nearly.

"Oh my God!" Dallas cries, tears running down her cheeks as she sprints towards us, her pack bouncing, her hair flying, the rifle in one hand.

She hits me like a linebacker and envelopes me in a hug, her wet cheek against my face.

"She shot you!" she says in between her half laughing, half crying. "I thought I'd have to... Well, I almost... I... I didn't... You..."

I hug her back tight and feel my own tears of relief, very aware that June is standing there watching, and likely much of Phantom Company; we are just across the bridge.

"Live dynamite," I whisper to her. "So, ahh... maybe don't hit me so hard next time."

She laughs, like I just told her a joke and then she disengages and Dallas and June are hugging and I breathe a sigh of relief. June hasn't experienced the last week with Dallas that I have, and I am glad to see them getting along.

They are both crying and I hear "thank yous" from both and then they are whispering. I let them be, dab at my head wound, it's almost done bleeding, so not bad at all, and go get my gear from under the mesquite tree.

I tie my jacket and suicide vest to the pack and get it on my back and look back at the Bright Angel Creek delta with Phantom Ranch beyond. It's nearly a perfect spot to be post-A. Maybe they'll get Talia under control, maybe they'll figure it out, but it's not the place for us.

As I'm looking, I see Harris standing in plain sight looking at us, his hands shoved in his pockets. Dallas told me that he was good with a rifle and was the one we'd have to watch out for. But he's not holding a rifle, he's just standing there, the noisy river between us.

June and Dallas are still talking but have started up the trail and I wave at Harris, and to my surprise he waves back with this half wave, half salute kind of thing.

He's going to honor the deal. I breathe a sigh of relief and catch up with the others.

When I get there, Dallas is saying to June, "...but I'm not sure what to think about it because after me, pantyhose are his next best friend."

My face flushes red.

"Pantyhose?" June asks, her eyes bright.

"Oh yeah," Dallas says with a mischievous smile. "He's a convert. Go ahead, Woody, show June your pantyhose."

They all stop, and with a sigh, I pull up one pant leg and they both laugh, and I just smile. Survival looks good for the day and there's the laughter. I'm okay with it being at my expense.

June gets a serious look on her face and examines my head. She makes me kneel down, takes off my hat, and wets my handkerchief and dabs at the wound. It hurts, but I've suffered worse, a lot worse.

"Not too deep," June says, her fingers gently moving my hair, "but you might need to change your part."

I thank her and we start back up the trail.

"Okay," Dallas says. "We need supplies, we need a destination, but first up, you two need a room."

My cheeks flush red again and I glance at June, but she's looking down as we walk up the dusty trail.

"I mean," Dallas continues, "if anyone, ever, in the history of mankind needed a room, it's you two. First June holds a gun to her head to save Woody, and then Woody nearly blows everyone up and gets shot in the head saving June and only survives because of June's jujitsu magic."

She stops and takes both of our hands, her brown eyes playful. "Don't be shy, kiddies, nod your heads and repeat after me. 'We need a room.'"

We both repeat after her quietly and she joins our hands together and slowly jogs up the trail. "Then let's find a room!" she shouts.

June and I stand there looking at each other; God, I do love those blue eyes of hers.

"Thank you," she says quietly.

I smile and nod. "Thank you." In one way, I'm saying thank you for saving my life again, but more than that I'm saying thank you for giving my lonely life meaning.

Maybe she can feel it too. It's a moment again. I could lean down and kiss her, all the emotions of the rescue still with us, the Grand Canyon surrounding us, the Colorado below. I'm about to lean down when...

"Come on!" Dallas shouts. "The sooner we get to the top, the sooner we can find that room you two so *clearly* need."

June shakes her head and smiles. "It's okay. We've got time, Woody. We've got time."

When we catch up, Dallas says to June, "So, did Diamondback here tell you about the secret scribblings he's been doing while pining away for you?" Dallas has a wicked smile playing on her lips and my cheeks flush red, yet again.

"Who's Diamondback?" June asks.

"Oh," Dallas says with a knowing nod. "That's the nickname Mr. Short and Stocky aka Asshole, real name Brown, gave our hero here."

She grabs my hat and puts it on her head. "On account of his ever-present baseball cap."

I feel naked without it, my overlong bangs falling into my eyes. I don't say a thing, I'm hoping the "scribblings" comment is ignored.

We fall into silence, hauling up the trail, the Colorado still near, and the bridge still in sight.

"Wait," June says. "What scribblings?"

"That was private," I say, snatching my hat back from Dallas and putting it on.

"Don't think so," Dallas says, clearly enjoying herself. "We are all in it."

"In what?" June's eyes are serious now.

"I've just... you know..." I stammer. "Been taking some notes on everything that's happened since we met. Writing a little bit."

June grabs my hand and stops me. She's blinking and her face flows through emotions quickly, from surprise, to puzzlement, to a shy smile. "Really?"

"Yeah. I... I didn't know if I'd ever get you back, and..." I can't think of anything else to say and just stand there getting lost in June's eyes.

"And tell her what you're calling it," Dallas whispers, suddenly close to us.

"Woody and June versus the Apocalypse," I say quietly.

June smiles widely and nods. "Are you going to write it?"

I shrug. "If we get the time, if I don't run out paper. Why not?"

She smiles, squeezes my hand, and we start walking back up the trail.

"But the title..." Dallas says. "You know... it's kind of lacking something."

"What?" I ask.

She stops in the trail, her hands on her hips shaking her head and then pointing at herself. "Woody and June and *Dallas* versus the Apocalypse."

I open my mouth to speak, but June speaks first. "No... No, I think it should be 'June and Dallas and Woody versus the Apocalypse.'"

"Yes!" Dallas yells, pumping her fist and heading back up the trail. "Majority rules, Woody, that's the title."

I stand there for a moment getting a glimpse of my future with these two women. It won't be easy, but it won't be boring, that's for sure.

"You know," I say as I catch up, "I can't put your name in the title, Dallas."

"Why not?" she asks.

"Really, you are the most interesting character. You appear to be a villain at first, but then you turn out to be crucial to our success. If I put your name in the title, that tension will be lost to the reader."

Everyone is silent for a moment and Dallas laughs, a full-bodied, echo-off-the-canyon-walls loud laugh. "You got the gift of bullshit, Woody, I'll give you that."

"That's not bullshit," I say. It's not. The story will be better if Dallas is a mystery.

"It's one of the things we love about you," June says with a smile.

I stand there as the two of them continue up the trail. "It's not bullshit!" I yell, but I am smiling. Yup, this is going to be interesting.

CHAPTER THIRTEEN

IT WAS dark when Dallas and I rolled into the South Rim and we were focused, so we didn't see much of anything. When the three of us make it out of the canyon, it's late afternoon and despite the pantyhose, my feet are killing me.

As we carefully explore the area, weapons out, we see what happened here.

The historic and sprawling El Tovar Hotel, constructed out of pine logs and Kaibab limestone, burned down. The rustic Bright Angel Lodge and cabins, another one of Mary Coulter's creations, has significant damage, doors bashed down, broken windows, and the bodies... there are a lot of them. Emaciated tourist zombies with bashed in heads, well chewed on corpses too far gone for the fungus to take over, signs of the living versus the undead everywhere.

"It was the horde," I say quietly as we stand on the rim near the remains of the El Tovar. The fireplaces, blackened limestone walls, and a few charred timbers remain, but the rest is a pile of ash. The breeze brings a whiff of the fire long gone.

June nods.

"We didn't come up here after we discovered the herd," Dallas says, her voice uncharacteristically quiet.

"The horde, it roamed the South Rim," I say, "and eventually got each group that set up here." I look at June. "We got lucky."

June takes my hand, nods, and squeezes my hand.

Our initial sweep is clear, and we start to scrounge and find it remarkably easy. These groups that came up here were well equipped, with vehicles and gas and food. In no time, we pick through and load the truck and crew cab with as much as it can carry, the bed loaded high and a cargo net thrown over it.

I even find a bat. It's aluminum, not wood, but I'll take it. I carry it over my shoulder after I find it, feeling a lot more like myself.

Afterwards we find that room. The decidedly not historic Thunderbird Lodge is in good shape. It was built in the late sixties out of brick with lots of windows and looks odd sandwiched between the wooden El Tovar and Bright Angel lodges.

Dallas sets up a room on the second floor and is very secretive about it and won't tell us anything until it's ready.

My breath catches when I walk in. It's got a spectacular view of the canyon and the sun is about to set, the darkening shadows making the Grand Canyon even more beautiful with colors ranging from dark grey to dark red, layer after layer of stone laid out before us.

She escorts us to a round table right by the windows and I pull the chair out for June and then sit across from her. The table has plates and forks and a cold can of chili, crackers, and dried fruit. What you would call a feast in the post-A world.

"One more thing," Dallas says, pulling something from behind the pillows of the king bed and hiding it behind her back. She has a huge smile on her face. I realize that this is the real Dallas. Those smile lines are earned, she is a woman that likes to be irreverent and loves to laugh, but can be remarkably caring. She pulls a bottle of champagne from behind her back and says, "Ta da!"

She produces two crystal goblets, pops the cork and pours.

"Warm, I know," she says, "but as the saying goes 'any champagne in an apocalypse.'"

She leaves the bottle and walks to the bed and pauses, her brow furrowed. Her expression turns to a smile and she pulls out another bottle of champagne, puts the new one on the table, and takes the open bottle. "I gotta have some fun," she says with a shrug and walks out of the room and closes the door.

Suddenly it's just June and me. And it's... sweet and shy and way too awkward.

We've been waiting to have our moment, and now that we have the space, the moment doesn't appear to be here. We caught up on the hike out, so what is there really to talk about?

"You look beautiful," I say. It's the only thing I can think of. We had enough water for us all to wash up a bit, but she always looks beautiful.

"Thank you," she says shyly, her hand straying to the bruise on her face. She takes the chili and portions it out. "You look very nice, too."

I smile and thank her. I combed my hair, trimmed my beard with some scissors we found, have a clean T-shirt on, and actually took my Diamondback's cap off.

I got a good look at my forehead when I cleaned up. The bullet grazed a path about an inch and a half long. I cleaned it as best I could, even found some hydrogen peroxide, but it's a scabby mess and I'm going to have an interesting scar. I feel a bit self-conscious about it, but this doesn't feel like the right time to be wearing my hat.

"To being alive and being together," I say holding my glass up, finding myself staring at the bubbles, suddenly feeling shy, wondering, yet again, if this thing between us is real.

"To being alive and being together," she says with a sniff.

I look up and she's crying and I'm pretty sure it's a good cry, but I still feel that desperate need to do something about it.

We hold the glasses there for far too long, just staring at each other and then I feel the tears sliding down my cheeks too. It's been three weeks and we've been through a lot. I feel not one bit of shame about those tears.

She clinks her glass against mine and we sip the warm champagne, which isn't that great, but the alcohol is a wonderful treat. Dallas is on watch—albeit with her own champagne—so we can actually relax.

And then the ice breaks and we're chatting. I'm telling her details about rafting down the Grand Canyon with Dallas and she's telling me about her slow campaign with Harris and Sal and Mary, and the knock-down, drag-out fight she had with Talia in front of the whole company.

"What started it?" I ask.

She shrugs. "I refused an order. It was a stupid order."

"Who won?"

She snorts. "Did you see her face?"

"To Talia getting her face punched," I say, holding my glass up. She clinks hers to mine, the sound like music.

Soon the food is gone and we're most of the way through the second bottle of champagne and I'm worried it's about to get awkward again.

"So what's next?" June asks.

"I have a plan..." I say with a big smile.

She smiles and shakes her head. "Well, let's have it, partner."

"I... I don't know," I say, touching my lips. "My lips are tired of talking right now. They need something... something soft, something sweet..."

My heart is pounding so hard I think she must be able to hear it.

"Soft? Sweet?" she asks, putting down her glass and getting up and walking over to me. She puts her finger on my lips. "Like this?"

I shake my head, but not enough to dislodge her finger. "Sweet, yes, but not soft enough."

"Hmmm," she says, looking around the room. "I might think you meant my lips, but mine are still pretty chapped." She picks up a napkin. "This?"

"Soft, but not at all sweet. And, by the way, chapped lips can be *very* soft."

"Really?" she asks, bending towards me, her sweet scent mingling with the smell of the soap she used. "I don't know."

"Yeah," I say, my breath coming faster. "My lips are chapped, too, and there is nothing better for chapped lips than another set of chapped lips."

"Well...."

And then she puts her hand on the back of my head and presses her lips to mine and...

And the world disappears. There is no apocalypse, pre or post. There are no psychotic, petty, wannabe warlords, or desperate fights for survival. There is only June and me and our lips and then our tongues and then our bodies.

We have our moment, finally, and many wonderful moments after in the room our best friend Dallas prepared for us.

ᛉᛉᛉ ᛉᛉ ᛉᛉᛉ

SUNRISE over the Grand Canyon is a gentle affair, with sunlight streaming in from the east, filtering through and filling the depths of the canyon with warm light. It's magic light, soft and gentle, making the reds darker and the taupes more yellow, the easterly faces of the pyramids and temples warming, the westerly sides remaining steeped in dark mystery.

June and I stand there holding hands in our room in the Thunderbird Lodge watching the silent play of light. We are packed and ready to go, but the sunrise moment is not one to be missed.

I sigh, my eyes flicking to the empty rim trail. Not one being, living or dead, out there, the black pavement littered with leaves and dust and sticks, weeds forcing their way through cracks, the detritus of time no longer swept away by park staff and the endless trodding of human feet. No more tourists here at one of the world's natural wonders.

"You okay?" June whispers, her hand squeezing mine.

I don't answer, my eyes going to a motion coming from the direction of the burned down El Tovar. My heart quickens and my maudlin moment is replaced by fear... of the living and the dead. But it's just a couple of mule deer meandering through the grass, munching their breakfast, their large ears flicking a bit as they listen for danger, their ribs showing under their brown/grey fur.

This is their canyon now.

"Yeah," I say, quietly, reverently. "It's so beautiful, it's just that..."

"Yeah," she echoes. I know she feels it too.

The scene itself seems to speak volumes about this new post-apocalyptic world. Nature is coming back and taking over as humanity recedes, holding on desperately for survival.

A few weeks ago, I was alone and desperate, but now my world, with June and Dallas in it, doesn't seem so much like an apocalypse anymore. Maybe, just maybe, things are turning around for us.

CHAPTER FOURTEEN

THE TRUCK IS PACKED tight as we head along the South Rim towards Desert View Overlook. The sun is shining and there are no Zs, and no psychotic, petty, wannabe warlords, just the three of us with more supplies than we've ever had.

The desert is lit by the sun's early morning orange-yellow glow making the world look almost friendly. I glance at June and can't help but smile, she catches my eye, smiles back, and then looks away.

"Oh, God!" Dallas says from the backseat. "Maybe that room wasn't such a good idea.

"I mean," she continues, "is this what it's going to be like from now on? You two all doey-eyed and mushy, me all alone and grumpy."

I open up my mouth to speak.

"No!" Dallas shouts. "No details, not a word. I'm going to die an unloved spinster, the last thing I need to hear is any details from you, young man."

I just smile as I drive, catching glimpses of the canyon to our left.

"And by no details," Dallas whispers to June loud enough that

I'm clearly meant to hear it, "I mean, tell me everything once we have some girl time. And I mean *everything*."

I glance at June, her cheeks are flushed, but there's a mischievous look in her face.

"I don't know," June says to Dallas. "I can't stand the thought of you a lonely, old, dried-up spinster. What can we do about that?"

There's a moment of silence and I swear the two of them are communicating telepathically or something, you can almost feel the unsaid words bouncing around the cab of the truck.

Dallas takes a deep breath and says, "Well, the only decent man left in the world is right here. You know, maybe..."

June finishes the sentence, "...maybe we can share him."

My eyes wide, I glance at June, who looks very mischievous now. Dallas's head is close to mine and I can hear her breathing. I look ahead and have to swerve hard because I almost ran us off the road. Both of them laugh.

"I mean, if humanity is to continue," Dallas says, "you have to face facts, Woody. You're going to have to get both of us pregnant and become the father of the new human race."

My hands are sweating on the steering wheel and my heart is pounding in my head. The images of "sharing" colliding with the images of crying babies and dirty diapers exploding in my head... and not in a good way.

"But...," June continues, "why not share all the way around? I mean, Dallas, you're the whole package, and I wouldn't mind..."

"Neither would I, honey," Dallas says. "Or, you know, all of us at once."

My brain is about to explode. I put Dallas firmly in the "sister" column during our quest to get June back. And now they're talking about sharing, and babies, and...

I slam on the brakes and bring us to a stop, the canyon visible to the left. "Are you guys being serious here, because... I... you know..." My cheeks are hot and I can't find the words.

They both laugh, it's a good laugh, free of restraint, truly joyful, and I know that laugh is coming at my expense, but I can live with that. Their faces are both bruised, Dallas's going to yellow at the edges and June's to purple. They need a good laugh, so I really *can* live with it.

"We might be..." Dallas begins.

"...but, honestly, I don't know that you're ready for it, even if we are," June ends.

"Yeah," Dallas adds. "I don't think he could handle the both of us."

Well, that is certainly true. I don't even know if I can handle June. Both of them still have smiles on their faces and I have no idea if they are serious, and no idea if I want them to be serious.

I nod slowly, looking into the blue eyes of June and then the brown eyes of Dallas. "You guys are just messing with me." I don't say it because I believe it, but because I need to focus. We've had a good laugh, now we need to survive.

"Sure... we're just messing with you," June says, that mischievous look still on her face, her tone leaving the question open.

"I think of you like a brother," Dallas says with a wide smile. "My little, snot-nosed brother, I might add, but a brother. Besides, as I told you before, Beckman, I'm nobody's second choice."

I take a deep breath and sigh, trying to shake free all the images floating around my head. "Okay, onward." I put the truck back into gear.

"So what's the plan?" Dallas asks.

"Yeah," June adds. "We... ah... didn't have time to talk about it last night."

"Details," Dallas stage whispers to June. "Later."

I shake my head, stop the truck, get the map out of my pocket, and get out. "I'll show you."

We found a good collection of maps when we were scrounging, and this one of Arizona is one of them. After looking around the desert landscape—trying to get my brain back into survival-first mode —I lay the map out on the warm hood of the truck.

"We're here." I point to Route 64 about halfway between the Grand Canyon Village and Desert View Overlook. "What we need is year-round running water, somewhere where we can grow food, somewhere remote."

"Where we can fish," Dallas adds.

"And horses would be good," June says. "I used to ride when I was a girl."

I smile, glad to see them focused. I run to the truck, grab my jacket, and pull the seed packets out. There are about eight of them in a plastic bag. Carrots, tomatoes, lettuce, a few varieties of beans. "Food," I say. "We need a place to grow food." I point at Sedona. "Oak Creek runs year-round, but too many people, which means too many Zs, and the ever-present psychotic, petty, wannabe warlords." I point southeast of Flagstaff. "Lake Mary is near Flagstaff, which is not a good place for us, and it's too cold."

They nod. Given our requirements, there are not a lot of places in Arizona that meet them and I'm worried about heading out of state, who knows what we might run into. At least I know Arizona.

"Anyone ever heard of the White Mountains or the Black River?" I point to eastern Arizona.

They both shake their heads.

"Mountains, lakes, rivers, and huge amounts of wilderness. We should be able to get lost there. There can't be that many Zs or that many psychotic, petty, wannabe warlords."

After I'm done, there's silence and the wind picks up, the sound of cawing ravens floating in on the breeze.

"That's a long ways to go," Dallas says quietly.

June points to the map, "And it looks like Flagstaff is the easiest way to get there."

"And we can't go through Flagstaff," I say. "Brown may have blown himself up, but he may not have."

Any city could have encampments, and unlike when I met June, we now have a lot of valuable stuff, a lot to lose.

Dallas slowly nods. "I can fish, get me there and we'll eat." We have fishing gear that we found on the South Rim.

"And if we can switch to horses on the way," June says, "we can stay away from people and keep moving."

"But how do we get there?" Dallas asks.

"Slowly. Carefully," I say, placing my hand on the map near the White Mountains.

"As a team," Dallas adds.

"Partners," June says, putting her hand on top of mine and Dallas does the same.

I look at them both and feel... Well, these things aren't simple, are they? I am quite sure that when we aren't in survival mode, I will be teased mercilessly, and while that will be uncomfortable, it will also be nice in a way. While I am in love with June, relationships are complicated in the best of times and these are not that. And then there is all the healing we need to do. Our bodies and our souls.

So I feel excited to be on a new adventure. I feel grateful to have such competent companions. And I feel scared and nervous for what me might face.

But I'm not alone. Underneath it all, I feel hope for a better future.

"Partners," I say, and then Dallas says the same and then all at once, together, we all say "Partners!"

We hug, I fold up the map, and June and Dallas get in the truck.

I stand there for a moment, looking down the road. I take off my Diamondbacks hat and finger the bullet hole and shake my head and feel... well, there is no getting around it, despite the challenges and the apocalypse, I feel happy.

I smile, put my hat back on and get in the truck. I put it in gear and head us towards our future.

MORE ADVENTURE?

There is so much more Woody and June (and Dallas too) coming. If you loved these stories (and if you got to the end here, I sure hope you did), please join the Woody and June Fan Club at WoodyAndJune.com, and for bonus points, tell everyone you know! The more support these books get, the faster I'll get to writing the next volume. And if you join the fan club it guarantees you won't miss a thing and you'll get exclusive behind-the-scene details and cool free stuff.

Until then, remember that your life is an adventure and no matter what current "apocalypse" is befalling you, love hard, be kind, and take it all in stride.

While you wait, you might be interested in my superhero / love story series: *Neutrinoman & Lightningirl: A Love Story*. In this series I take a similar spin on the superhero genre as I did here with zombies. Real characters in extraordinary situations that are full of adventure, fun, and romance. Season 1 is out, with Season 2 coming soon. All the details are below.

SUPERHEROES... FALLING IN LOVE... SAVING THE WORLD.

Follow Nik Nichols (aka Neutrinoman) and Licia Lopez (aka Lightningirl) on this wild adventure past "happily ever after" into the heart of love while they try to protect the Earth from aliens bent on our destruction.

Join my newsletter and get the *Meteor Attack!* ebook for free!

Meteor Attack!: *Falling in love and saving the world...*

Toxic Asset: *Friend or Enemy?*

Protocol X: *An Alien Encounter*

Season 1: *Episodes 1-3 for a great price!*

Find out more about the series at Neutrinoman.com

ABOUT THE AUTHOR

Robert J. McCarter is the author of six novels, three novellas, and dozens of short stories. He is a finalist for the *Writers of the Future* contest and his stories have appeared in *The Saturday Evening Post, Adomeda Spaceways Inflight Magazine, Everyday Fiction,* and numerous anthologies.

He has written a series of first person ghost novels (starting with Shuffled Off: A Ghost's Memoir) and a superhero / love story series (Neutrinoman and Lightningirl, A Love Story), as well as two short story collections.

Of his latest novel, *Seeing Forever,* Kirkus Reviews says, "Sci-fi as it should be: engaging, moving, and grand in scope."

Find out more at:
robertjmccarter.com

BOOKS BY ROBERT J. MCCARTER

WOODY AND JUNE VERSUS THE APOCALYPSE

1. Woody and June versus the Wannabe Warlord
2. Woody and June versus the Fungus-Head Zombies
3. Woody and June versus the Grand Canyon
4. Woody and June versus the Ex
5. Woody and June versus the Third Wheel
6. Woody and June versus Phantom Company (*coming August, 2019*)
7. Woody and June versus the Daring Rescue (*coming September, 2019*)

Join the Woody and June Fan Club at WoodyAndJune.com

NOVELS IN THE "GHOST'S MEMOIR" WORLD:

- Shuffled Off: A Ghost's Memoir, Book 1
- Drawing the Dead
- To Be a Fool: A Ghost's Memoir, Book 2
- Of Things Not Seen: A Ghost's Memoir, Book 3

OTHER NOVELS:

- Seeing Forever

BOOKS IN THE NEUTRINOMAN AND LIGHTNINGIRL SERIES:

- Meteor Attack! Neutrinoman and Lightningirl, A Love Story. Episode 1
- Toxic Asset: Neutrinoman and Lightningirl, A Love Story. Episode 2
- Protocol X: Neutrinoman and Lightningirl, A Love Story. Episode 3
- Season 1 (Omnibus edition of Episodes 1 - 3)
- Off Book: Neutrinoman and Lightningirl, A Love Story. Episode 4 (*Coming soon*)

WALTER ANCHOR, GHOST DETECTIVE STORIES

- **Case 1: "Detecting Haley"** (part of *Life After: Stories of Life, Death, and the Places in Between*)
- **Case 2: "The Ghost Brides Gift"** (exclusive to newsletter subscribers)
- **Case 3: "A Long Hard Fall"** (coming in 2019)

For a complete list of Walter Anchor stories, go to RobertJMcCarter.com/WalterAnchor

SHORT STORES AND COLLECTIONS

- Life After: Stories of Life, Death, and the Places in Between
- Anomalous Readings: Thirteen Curious and Confounding Tales
- Probability: Resolve
- The Turing Test Will Be Televised

- Ghost Hacker, Zombie Maker

For a complete list, go to RobertJMcCarter.com